# Tiny Treasures

## TALES FROM GREAT BRITAIN

First published in Great Britain in 2010 by
Young Writers, Remus House, Coltsfoot Drive,
Peterborough, PE2 9JX
Tel (01733) 890066 Fax (01733) 313524
Website: www.youngwriters.co.uk

# Foreword

Since Young Writers was established in 1990, our aim has been to promote and encourage written creativity amongst children and young adults. By giving aspiring young authors the chance to be published, Young Writers effectively nurtures the creative talents of the next generation, allowing their confidence and writing ability to grow.

With our latest fun competition, *The Adventure Starts Here* ..., primary school children nationwide were given the tricky challenge of writing a story with a beginning, middle and an end in just fifty words.

The diverse and imaginative range of entries made the selection process a difficult but enjoyable task with stories chosen on the basis of style, expression, flair and technical skill. A fascinating glimpse into the imaginations of the future, we hope you will agree that this entertaining collection is one that will amuse and inspire the whole family.

# Contents

# The Mini Sagas

# Colosseum

Watching in the hot colosseum, people are cheering and the Emperor is happy. Blood is shooting out of the gladiators. Swords are waving and gladiators are staring. They are growling, standing straight. It is very noisy! One dies, the other is the winner and the Emperor is proud of him.

**Harrison Scott (7)**

# The Mary Rose's Last Voyage

*Bang!* Cannonballs hit the decks, wood splinters
into the faces of soldiers. Ferociously, water
torments the ship. Masts crash, slicing the deck in
half. The weary sails follow, covering the deck like
a blanket, knowing the end is nigh.
Opening the door, light streams through the Mary
Rose exhibit.

**Tom Lawson (11)**

# The Long Tunnel!

Caramel was crawling through a very long tunnel for what seemed to be hours. She thought she was getting nowhere! Her feet and her hands ached terribly. All of a sudden Caramel saw light and reached the end and realised that she was still in her large cage under heaps of sawdust!

**Ellie Green (9)**

# The Sound On The Roof

It was a snowy night and I was in bed. I heard a big thump on the roof and a sound that sounded like hooves trotting. I ran down the stairs and at the mince pie that I had left out, there was a bite mark in it …

**Daniel Ashton (10)**

# The Haunted House Of Doom

As Bill opened the door and entered the house, a ghost jumped on him. Vampires were surrounding him. He screamed, 'Argh!' The house was too dark to go anywhere. Then his friends jumped out of nowhere, disguised as spiders and said, 'Haha, it's a trick!'

**Ridwan Madarbukus (9)**

# Football Match

I was at the stadium now but there were no people there. I was the only person in the whole stadium, but suddenly everyone jumped from the entrance doors and scared me. People were noticing that there was no referee. That's when the game became rough.

**Rayyan Madarbukus (9)**

# The Shoe Stealer

I went shopping with my friends. I picked up a shoe that I love. I asked the till manager if they had it in a size three, the person at the till was about to reply when a lady tapped me on the shoulder and said,
'Actually, that's my shoe!'

**Lois Horton-Giblin (9)**

# One World One Man

'Bill! Where are you? Come out!' Yelled Josh.
'Argh! Help!' Josh went running over to a large
hole in the ground.
'Josh help!' Bill was being pulled away by …
tentacles. Bill was gone …
'Mum, Dad, help!' Mum and Dad were gone! Josh
was the only one left. 'No, no, no!'

**Josh Allen (11)**
Bearbrook Combined School, Aylesbury

# The Dark Lord's Revenge

Danger struck as the Dark Lord's power was getting stronger than ever! His power grew as he was draining a helpless boy's powers. Then the helpless boy felt a dark connection coming deep inside an archway, the helpless boy heard noises coming from the dark archway, voices calling him …

**Cody Hayden (11)**
**Bearbrook Combined School, Aylesbury**

# The Park Mystery ...

*Eeek.* I opened the park gate. Slowly I walked in. I mumbled, 'I'm sure they said twelve fifty.' I looked at my watch, 12.50. 'Where are they then?' I said to myself. *Bang!* It hit me ... 'Oh thank God!' It was only the ball. 'Now it's time to play football.'

**Thomas Daly (11)**
**Bearbrook Combined School, Aylesbury**

# Dream!

'Kelly, Kelly, Kelly.' Went the wind, whispering her name … Kelly stuck to her bed, she said, 'Who is this?' Then she saw someone at the end of the bed …

'I've been waiting for you to come back.' Then she screamed. She awoke and said, 'I hope that was a dream?'

**Sahrena Suffield (10)**
**Bearbrook Combined School, Aylesbury**

# The Weird Haunted House

Breathing fast, I crept up the ghostly stairs.
*Bang ... Bang ... Bang ...* Who or what was it?
A silhouette ran across the wall. *Bang!* A flash of
lightning hit the house. The silhouette vanished!
Then all of a sudden Supercat landed in the house
and telported me to my awesome home!

**Kingsley Parker (11)**
**Bearbrook Combined School, Aylesbury**

*12*

# When It Came!

Thunder crackling, lightning flashing and the wind whispering names of the dead ... *Knock, knock, knock* went the door! Who could it be? I went down the stairs to answer it! The door creaked open as a shiver ran down my spine! It was Violet, my cute and fluffy German Shepherd!

**Shafaq Imran (11)**
**Bearbrook Combined School, Aylesbury**

# Are They Zombies?

*Flash, bang, boom,* the stormy night was grumpy.
Sneakily I walked in the abandoned church next
to the graveyard. Outside the church something
was there … I could see amber red lights flashing
around. But it was only old Mr Jones on his
motorbike. *Knock knock.* 'Guys it's me, hello?'

**Daniel Pullen (10)**
Bearbrook Combined School, Aylesbury

# Beach Blues

'Yay!' I yelled. Finally we got to the beach. I
jumped out of the car, grabbed my beach towel
and went to build a sandcastle. But, as I sat down,
it started to rain. Oh no! I ran back to the car and
jumped inside. We had to go home.

**Gemma Cheng (11)**
**Bearbrook Combined School, Aylesbury**

# The Dragon King

In the musty skies stood a mountain. Legend had
it that at the top of the peak stood … The king
of dragons! He was the 'big boy', no one would
mess with him, so why turn around? As the sword
flew through his tough skin he bled. He was dead!

**Ryan Stevens (11)**
**Bearbrook Combined School, Aylesbury**

# Oh Brother!

'Help!' I shouted. Something was chasing me!
What was it? Running as fast as I could, too scared
to look back, the light flickered, I didn't have a
clue what to do but carried on running. I tripped,
I saw it. It was macabre. It was my annoying
brother!

**Majeed Ullah (10)**
**Bearbrook Combined School, Aylesbury**

17

# It's Getting Closer

*Tap, tap, tap* was the eerie sound I heard at my window. Something was out there ... *click!* The front door opened! *Thump, thump.* It was on the stairs and ... it was getting closer! My heart was pounding. Sleepwalking, it was only my foolish sister, snoring like a pig! Typical.

**Chloe Smith (11)**
**Bearbrook Combined School, Aylesbury**

# One, Two, Three ...

Josh and George were playing hide-and-seek.
George was counting and Josh was hiding. Josh
hid. 'Argh!' George ran inside. 'Mum, Dad I think
Josh went into the shed.'
'Oh no!' Said mum and Dad. They all ran outside.
'Are you still there?'
'Goodbye!'
'Josh, Josh.'
Josh died!

**Bibi Azara (10)**
**Bearbrook Combined School, Aylesbury**

# The Disappearances At The Terminal

Matthew walked through the airport towards the riot, he was a security guard and there was a riot in terminal 5. 'Calm down, calm down!' Matthew shouted. Suddenly all the lights went off. There was a crash. 'Argh!' screamed Matthew. Everyone had disappeared and an airliner was there instead.

**Jamie Winfield (11)**

Bearbrook Combined School, Aylesbury

# And Then We Heard The Bomb

The sirens were screaming. We all ran to the
exit doors out of the classrooom but they were
locked from the outside! We all ran back and
wondered what to do now. We decided to hide
under the tables, then we heard the Luftwaffe …
And then we heard the bomb!

**Shaun Nolan (11)**
**Bearbrook Combined School, Aylesbury**

21

# The Death

He walks, the wind blows, the night is dead …
No light, no life, no hope … The heart is gone
… He leaves a bloody trail … The scythe drips
with raw, ripping, oozing blood! Dead, cold,
gone forever. A phospherant jacket … He fights
through the wind … The Reaper is gone!

**Matthew Nicholls (10)**
Bearbrook Combined School, Aylesbury

# Evil Devil

*Bang, bang!* There was a knock on the door. Beth was all by herself. Her heart was pounding like mad. *bang!* The lights turned off. It was pitch-black. Beth couldn't see anything … The door opened.
'Boo!'
'Argh! Susan you little devil!'
'What it's just a joke!'

**Jessica Haden-Pound (11)**
**Bearbrook Combined School, Aylesbury**

# The Boy Who Cried Two-Headed Bear

A little boy came to our village. One day everyone said he lied. Every day he cried, 'Help! A two-headed bear is coming.' His mum didn't believe him.

Months passed by and he kept crying. 'A two-headed bear.' Suddenly a two-headed bear came and ate his mother!

**Lucy French (10)**
Bearbrook Combined School, Aylesbury

# See A Deep Blue Eye?

A girl called Grace kept on getting bullied by her annoying next-door neighbours. But then a miracle came to her, they moved to China! Since they've moved she has been seeing deep blue eyes! Voices are in her head and they'll never go away ... Never!

**Rachel Castillo (11)**
**Bearbrook Combined School, Aylesbury**

# Disappearing

Once a family went for a trot in the woods. They came across a deep, smelly, dirty river. The two kids put their fingers in the river. They heard a roar and sprinted to their mum. They both started to cry. A beast came out. They were never seen again.

**Tehmina Ahmad (11)**

Bearbrook Combined School, Aylesbury

# The Life Of A Dog Called Major

Yawning, he stretched his strong legs and his
bulging head. He shook his body and ran for
his ball, stopping on his way he looked for his
breakfast, it wasn't there! He barked immediately,
his owner poured his breakfast, *chomp!* It was
gone. After that he climbed back into bed.

**Oliver Scales (10)**
**Bearbrook Combined School, Aylesbury**

27

# The Spooky Castle

Cautiously I crept through the spooky castle.
There were cobwebs and dust everywhere. Then
all of a sudden I heard movement from upstairs,
and saw a great big transparent ghost. It started
to move about and then just disappeared!

**Nikkita Suffield (11)**

Bearbrook Combined School, Aylesbury

28

# Miss Lunn And The Monster

Miss Lunn was at school waiting for the children
to come back from the cloakroom. Then the
door creaked open, Miss Lunn was getting scared
and didn't know what to do. she decided to ask
'Is anyone there?'
'Hello,' the monster replied. Miss Lunn's heart
dropped dead …

### Maimoonah Afzal (10)
**Bearbrook Combined School, Aylesbury**

# Last Vampire Standing

Saturday morning, I was walking down 5th Street.
A limo pulled up, a person lured me inside, it was
full of people with red eyes and razor sharp teeth.
One dashed at me. I moved my head. It bit me.
The moment I got bitten I entered a new race.

**Tyrique Williams (11)**
**Bearbrook Combined School, Aylesbury**

# Little Red Riding Hood: The Retelling

One lovely, cloudless day Little Red Riding Hood was riding through the Grim Forest on her flourescent bicycle. A bloodthirsty wolf was watching her hungrily. As she reached her grandma's the wolf jumped out … Quietly, a burly axeman chopped the wolf grotesquely in half … But it survived. 2 snacks. Yum!

**Benjamin Hutchinson (11)**
**Bearbrook Combined School, Aylesbury**

# Bang!

Once there was a dog called Zulu, with his owner
Lutin, who went to the field …
Finally they were at the field. Lutin brought some
balloons with him for an important experiment …
*bang!* Zulu got what he wanted, he popped all the
balloons!

**Lutin Smuts (11)**
Bearbrook Combined School, Aylesbury

32

# Ghostly Goings-On

Anxiously, Pat crept to the front door. He tapped
the knocker. No answer, although he could hear a
shrieking and clanging inside. What was going on?
He peeped through the letterbox. An eerie figure
swept down the stairs, towards the door. *Creak!*
The door opened … Then the Halloween party
began.

**Robert Thompson (10)**
**Bearbrook Combined School, Aylesbury**

# A Day In The Life Of Jacob

Jacob woke up every morning and went to watch TV or play his Xbox. However all that changed when he was talent-spotted playing football. However he gave that sport up because he missed his Xbox too much.
Now he is Xbox champion of the world. Hooray for Jacob.

**Jacob Ayres (11)**
**Bearbrook Combined School, Aylesbury**

# The Boy And Girl

There was a boy and his girlfriend. He was called
Callum and she was called Tanya. One day they
were walking and saw an old house. They saw
some witches' brooms. The witches were hiding.
They grabbed them and nearly poisoned them …

**Mairi MacKenzie (9)**
**Darvel Primary School, Darvel**

# The Hostage

A wee boy and his friend went to the loch. They met some older boys who gave them sweets. After that they were sick all over the wall. They went home and the older boys brought them some soup and went back outside to play. They hurt themselves.

**Calum Steel (9)**
Darvel Primary School, Darvel

36

# Best Birthday Ever

As she woke, Lydia became more excited. Today was her 10th birthday. She quickly ripped open her presents, changed into her new riding clothes, grabbed her crop and hat and set off in her dad's Mazda RX5. She arrived at Grassyards Livery Yard. Lydia bought a horse called Pepstar Pepe.

**Abby Fraser (9)**
**Darvel Primary School, Darvel**

# The Nightmare

James was in a deserted house. He thought he was at home but his parents were not there. He heard a noise in the kitchen like knives dropping on the floor. James went to the kitchen but suddenly something grabbed him!
He woke up and was relieved. 'Mum!' shouted James.

**Jamie McKendrick (10)**
**Darvel Primary School, Darvel**

# Alone In The Dark

One dark night, Abby came home from work.
When Abby arrived home the house looked
deserted. Her mum and dad were meant to be
home. Abby went to her friend Sarah's house to
give her a present. It was cold, then Abby fainted.
Sarah took her inside the house.

**Amy Pollock (9)**
**Darvel Primary School, Darvel**

# Don't Mess With Mum

Jim was at Tom's house and Mum said she was going to work. Then they saw her purse and went down the street with it. They bought sweets. Five hours later Mum came back and saw the boys on the main road, so she took them home to ground them.

**Ryan Harrison (9)**
**Darvel Primary School, Darvel**

# 1970s

One sunny Saturday morning, during the 1970s, it was a fabulous day because my papa was going to see the Bay City Rollers at the concert hall. My papa was singing Shang-a-lang! After the concert, he walked home and thought what a super night it was!

**Tariq Murdoch (9)**
**Darvel Primary School, Darvel**

# Halloween Blackout

One dark, murky Halloween, Jim was sitting watching TV when suddenly … the TV turned off and everything went quiet. Jim got his mobile phone and tried to call the electrician but his phone was out of money. He went outside and then everybody jumped out shouting, 'Happy Halloween!'

**Ruaridh Hopkins (9)**
**Darvel Primary School, Darvel**

42

# On Holiday

One sunny day in Spain, Lucy and her big sister went to a water park. They went on the black hole ride, they raced and felt excited. With a splash, Lucy won! At last they got their lunch and thought that was the most super and wonderful day ever.

**Alice Yeudall (10)**

**Darvel Primary School, Darvel**

# The Evil Petshop

'I don't like the look of that gerbil, Mum,' I said.
'Don't worry,' said Mum. 'It's not a monster,' she
said.
'They've got the wrong idea …' squeaked the
gerbil. Roar! The gerbil chased Mum out the
shop.
'Mum, where are you?'

**Kyle Anderson (9)**
**Darvel Primary School, Darvel**

# Grizzly Hamster

Once, a little girl called Angela bought a little,
cute, fluffy hamster. Then one day she was
letting him crawl around the floor while she was
cleaning out the cage. She went to get food but
the hamster was a grizzly bear and ate her. She
screamed, 'Argh!'

**Sarah Murray (9)**
**Darvel Primary School, Darvel**

# The Mirror On The Wall

When Bugs Bunny was walking home, he walked past the shrieking shack and decided to have a look inside. Then when he walked in he saw a glass mirror which had a *For Sale* sign on it. Bugs leaned in, the mirror began to speak. Bugs Bunny was very amazed.

**Lucy Park (10)**
**Darvel Primary School, Darvel**

# The Forbidden Forest

One day Harry was walking through the forest when he heard a strange noise. It was like sticks cracking so he turned round and standing behind him was a giant werewolf! He ran for his life to get home. He turned the corner, he was safe and sound again.

**Emily Mair (10)**
**Darvel Primary School, Darvel**

# The Tiny Little Fairy

One day a girl answered her door but there was no one there. Then she shut the door and she heard it again. So she just left the door open and the doorbell rang again and again. So she kept looking outside. Then she saw a tiny little fairy.

**Amy McLean (10)**
Darvel Primary School, Darvel

# Up In The Loft

One day Henry was in the loft and all at once the
door shut, the light flickered and went out. He
didn't have a torch with him. He started to panic.
He got up and saw a beam of light. He headed
towards it. Then he saw his dad, *phew!*

**Craig Cochrane (9)**
Darvel Primary School, Darvel

# Swimming In The Ocean

One sunny day in the USA, a boy called Jambo
went and bought a surfboard and went down
to the ocean. He attempted to surf but then he
thought he saw a shark. He said, 'Oh no!' He
jumped quickly back on the board and headed
back to the land.

**Conor McIvor (9)**
**Darvel Primary School, Darvel**

# At A Farm

One day I was at a farm and there was a dog in
the field chasing some sheep and biting them.
Three sheep were hurt and we thought they
were dead.
I went up the farm the next day and they were
not dead. They had sore legs, and injuries.

**Tony Fagg (9)**
**Darvel Primary School, Darvel**

# Craig Out For The Count

One day I was playing football with my friend and I tripped up over a stick. I fell into a hole. When I woke up I saw some foxes and badgers and they spoke to me. So I crawled up the hole and went home and told my dad.

**Craig Roney (9)**
**Darvel Primary School, Darvel**

# The Dream Of Mirrors

One day a boy was walking down the street.
Suddenly he saw a mirror house that was never
there before. He barged the door open. When
he was inside, the door slammed shut. He looked
around, then a dragon smashed through the glass
of a mirror.
He woke up screaming!

**Connor Armstrong (11)**
**Darvel Primary School, Darvel**

# Monster In The Dark

Once there was a boy called Callum. He was
putting his jacket in the closet when he saw a
scary face and body with blood, wrinkles and lots
more things. Callum found out that it was a clown
face and a jacket. Callum felt so relieved but so
silly.

**Cameron McColl (9)**
**Darvel Primary School, Darvel**

# In The Castle

One day Sindy was at home and she decided to go on an adventure to the castle. She heard a noise and the door moved. A ghost was looking at her so she ran up the stairs. It was dark and she was very scared, in the castle alone.

**Adele Laing (10)**
**Darvel Primary School, Darvel**

# World's End

One dark night a boy called Jimmy went to sleep.
The next morning Jimmy woke up and looked out
his window. No one was to be seen. He ran to
his mum's bedroom, his mum wasn't there. He
went outside but there was no sign of life, except
friendly robots.

**Taylor Wolschke (9)**
**Darvel Primary School, Darvel**

# The Deserted Island

One dark, spooky night, James was on a deserted
island! James said in a low whispering voice,
'Hello, anybody there?'
Somebody replied in a quiet voice. 'I'm over here
in my cave.' So James walked over to the cave in
the middle of the jungle. 'Hi, I'm Jim.'
'I'm James.'

**Ryan Goudie (9)**
**Darvel Primary School, Darvel**

# Aliens Meet The Humans

Once upon a time there was a young girl called
Sophia who was an alien hunter. She had a phone
line and she got a call from two kids called Emma
and Ryan. They found an alien in their garden and
they were terrified. So Sophia went and killed it.

**Emma Louise McKinnon (10)**
Darvel Primary School, Darvel

# Halloween

The doorbell rang and Kerr looked out the letter box, then he opened the door. There was a gang of six people. 'Sweets please.' Then he realised it was just a bunch of kids. Kerr went to get the sweetie jar, he threw sweets into the air.

**Jack Henderson (9)**
**Darvel Primary School, Darvel**

# Untitled

One day Sam went on a sleepover at his friend's
house - Dan. They stayed up all night and Sam
was ready to set off on a trip to the dark forest.
But a big problem happened in the forest, a man
got killed there, and he had set off now.

**Conor Dyer (10)**
Greysbrooke Primary School, Lichfield

# The Fiery Dragon

I saw a dragon, it was as red as fire; it was as fast as a bullet, it was as light as a feather, it was even made of paper. Then it went away. Afterwards it turned into a page with lots of words, it was a book, after all.

**Alexander Capper (11)**
**Greysbrooke Primary School, Lichfield**

# Coming Home

The sun was hot in the sky as I trudged down
the road. My arms were aching from carrying my
school bag. I finally reached my house, sighing as I
felt in my bag for the key. I opened the door and
stared inside. 'Hello?' I called. It was empty.

**Ella Scharaschkin (10)**
Greysbrooke Primary School, Lichfield

# 50 Word Story

He climbed the steep steps to the party, then a ghost grabbed him and took him into a dungeon. 'You didn't tell me it was fancy dress,' said the boy. Then they both went back on ground level and enjoyed the party with all their friends from school.

**Peter Olliffe (11) & Theo**
**Greysbrooke Primary School, Lichfield**

# Stories, Who Needs Them!

I really hate making up stories. I'm just no good. Can't it be about maths? I'm really good at that, like making a formula or something or other. Why does life have to revolve around literacy? Why, why? Even my little sister is better than me, she's in Year 4.

**Georgina Bird**

Greysbrooke Primary School, Lichfield

# Untitled

It was the sunniest day of the year and we saw something in the bush in our garden, my mum said that I was daydreaming. I saw a head and I said, 'Hello, is anyone there?' I was terrified. Mum went in the bush, what happened … ?

**Lydia Starkey**
Greysbrooke Primary School, Lichfield

# The Goblin

The girl ran down the road, screaming from
a green goblin. She turned sideways, an alley.
She ran and ran but then she saw a dead end.
The goblin caught up with her! she screamed in
horror. 'Help, please!' But then the goblin said,
'Trick or treat? Ha, ha, ha!'

**Reece Smith (10)**
Hawkesley Church Primary School, Kings Norton

# A Special Surprise

She stopped and stared at the wall. She turned
around. A man was chasing her with a sword in
his hand. He had finally found her. She froze. The
man came closer. She thought he would steal her
money, but he came to say, 'I'm your brother.'
She was astonished.

**Samantha Hensey (11)**
**Hawkesley Church Primary School, Kings Norton**

# Dreaded Escape Route

Panting through the forest, shadows streamed from every corner. Gunfire thundered into my ears, following every move that I made. Footsteps grew harder, clambered along, approaching closer towards me. Heart accelerated, feet came into overdrive, getting away from it. I had won the gold trophy and was proud.

**Johnathan Beckford (11)**

**Hawkesley Church Primary School, Kings Norton**

# Dentist Darkness

Drilling, sawing and loud screams were in the room. David shook like a tumble dryer on full speed. The man came out the room with a drill. David shook even more. 'Next please,' the dentist insisted.

**Sophia Zaib (10)**
Hawkesley Church Primary School, Kings Norton

# The Underground Escape

The walls were shaking, the floor was trembling.
It was cold and my teeth were chattering. I stood
nervously, waiting. Waiting people crowd. The
screams became noisier and louder, the noise
pierced my ears. I started to shake, I felt like I was
an ice cube. Instantaneously the train arrived.

**Lydia Hinchley (11)**
Hawkesley Church Primary School, Kings Norton

# Redditch Travel

'Bye Mum,' I shouted while I jogged off to the
bus stop. As I bumped into a man … I ran to the
bus and leapt on. I hopped off and ran as fast
as lightning to JD. Back on bus, long travel …
Suddenly I see the man again …

**Chloe Welsh (11)**
Hawkesley Church Primary School, Kings Norton

# Disaster Strikes

She could hear scratching and knocking on the
neighbour's door. It meant she was next in line.
She heard loud footsteps heading towards her.
*Ding-dong!* She opened the door nervously,
horrific sound greeted her. 'Trick or treat?' a little
boy whispered.

**Caitlan Hall (10)**
Hawkesley Church Primary School, Kings Norton

# The Scaly Monster

The door burst open, a scaly creature approached me. He looked at me with his beady eyes. I couldn't escape from the treacherous walls of the dungeon, blood dripping from the plate. My grandad said to me, 'Do you want any jam tarts?'

**Ashley Field (11)**
Hawkesley Church Primary School, Kings Norton

# Sweet Sixteen

I was at school with my friends and we were chatting about our sweet sixteen. My friend Chloe said she is having a massive party and a sleepover. Kayleigh said she's having her party on a boat with lots of balloons and I said, 'I'm having a pink Hummer.'

**Katie Connor (11)**
Hawkesley Church Primary School, Kings Norton

# The Crazed Killer

His blood-red eyes filled with rage. His
sledgehammer was lifted and … blood was
splattered over his face. After, a mighty demon
came. The killer said, 'So you have finally come to
face me!'
'I will kill you for killing my brother.' Then a
power cut, the game was over.

**Connor Hogan (11)**
Hawkesley Church Primary School, Kings Norton

# Dangerous Adventure

One early morning, I had a dream I would have dangerous adventures with powerful dragons and play a trick on Mom. Firstly, escape to the country. Secondly, gather the money. Thirdly, buy a packed lunch, and nothing could stop me! A strange shadow came from a bush. Was it Mom?

**Tyreak Brown (10)**
Hawkesley Church Primary School, Kings Norton

# Sharkman

Sharkman was captured by a fishing boat. He was
stuck. He ripped the rope, bit someone's leg and
jumped into the water. He thought he was safe
but he wasn't. The police boats came, started
shooting at him. Blood surged upwards then, the
body of Sharkman bobbed above water.

**Brandon Weeks (11)**

**Hawkesley Church Primary School, Kings Norton**

# The Killer Squirrel

As the car sped up the street Johnny heard
scratching at the car window. 'Argh!' screeched
Emily. Johnny went over 70. All of a sudden the
car stopped. 'What will we do?' asked Emily. Just
then the car window smashed. A squirrel grabbed
some popcorn and ran off.

**Bethany Chambers (11)**
**Hawkesley Church Primary School, Kings Norton**

# Scary Nightmare

I was on my way to a rich school, when a professor kidnapped me. I kicked him and he cried, he was a scaredy-cat. I was laughing my head off, then I stole his car and drove to school, I knew I would be safe and sound.

**Liam Wilcox (10)**
Hawkesley Church Primary School, Kings Norton

# Trying To Escape

When I went to school yesterday, my friends were there. Mrs James locked us in the cupboard until lunchtime. After lunch we went back in there. Mrs James went home. We needed to get out.

Thursday came. Everybody came to school, we were still in the cupboard.

**Glen Bennett (11)**

Hawkesley Church Primary School, Kings Norton

# The Gloomy Day

One gloomy day in Toy Town, the sky was a dull grey. Suddenly big claps of thunder came down from the sky. Instantly lightning came down from the sky. It set fire to the trees. All that was left was an incredible flower. It was a gloomy, horrible day.

**Katie-Anne Jane McCarthy (10)**
**Hawkesley Church Primary School, Kings Norton**

# Mine And Joe's Adventure

I was trapped by gorillas and Joe was risking his
life for me. I could not defend myself. They had
a smart machine. So Joe disguised into a really
strong gorilla. Next he went to the gorillas and
killed them all, then he saved me.

**Brendon Notley (11)**
Hawkesley Church Primary School, Kings Norton

# One Little Wolf And The Big Bad Pig

There was one little wolf that left his mother to live on his own. The wolf made his house from straw. Opposite his house was a bad pig. The pig wanted to eat the wolf. He caught the wolf and ate him in one massive gulp!

**Ayah Alzetani (9)**

**Pearl Hyde School, Coventry**

# One Day In My Life: Elizabeth I

I went to Mary and declared she would be
beheaded, and with that one word, her head
dropped and that was the last of her!
A feast began and lasted all night. There was
everything I needed, music, laughter and dance.
The evening finished and I fell asleep.

**Vismaya Jose (9)**
**Pearl Hyde School, Coventry**

# Midnight Horror

Corly came home, there was a sudden crack
and whistle, and then suddenly there was a
knock at the door. Corly didn't answer. 'Argh!'
she shrieked. 'Oooo, Oooo. There was another
knock at the door. There was an instant shriek,
the door opened, it was Mum. 'Oh Mum!'

**Autumn Stevens-Minns (8)**

**Pearl Hyde School, Coventry**

# The Winning Goal

Today was the big final. The game kicked off.
The game was close and the score was even.
With minutes left I was fouled. It was a penalty,
I stepped up and kicked the ball into the back of
the net, the team celebrated as we had won the
cup.

**Owen Ashby (8)**

**Pearl Hyde School, Coventry**

# Bradsterion And The Giro

At the time of the Ancient Greeks, there lived
a prince called Bradsterion. He was going to be
king but his uncle took the throne. To get the
throne back Bradsterion had to kill the Giro.
Bradsterion accepted the challenge and won the
throne. He was crowned king for evermore.

**Bradley Gough (8)**
Pearl Hyde School, Coventry

# The Nine Lives Of Billy

Billy was a cat, he was cute. He had nine lives.
He spent them very quickly. He was starting to
get weak. He was taken to the vet. The vet had
bad news. Billy was going to die. But when he got
home he was strong. Everyone was happy.

**Alice Hillary (8)**

Pearl Hyde School, Coventry

# Sophie's Dress

Sophie wanted to wear her new dress. Her mum said, 'Yes!' She wanted to play outside. So her friends could see it. She did a cartwheel and fell over. Oh dear, there was a hole in her dress, so her mum kindly mended it, although she was cross!

**Rachel Cooper (7)**
**Pearl Hyde School, Coventry**

# The Confused Man

Ah, almost tidy. *Ding-dong.* Who is it?
*'Woooo!'*
TV turns on. 'Hello, who's there?'
*Crash, bang!*
'Sorry about the damage, but there happens to
be a ghost in your house. By the way we're Ghost
Busters, look there he is.'
Zzz
'He's captured. Let's go.'
'I'll fix my door!'

**Ammaar Sultan (9)**
Pearl Hyde School, Coventry

# Ghosts

*Knock, knock.* 'Huh? What was that?' the boy said.
'Nothing.'
*Ding-dong.*
He crept to the door, he got his goo shooter and
flung open the door. 'On guard!' he shouted.
'Whoo.' It was a ghost! Quickly he sprayed goo at
it, but it was just the postman.

**Partha Joshi (9)**
**Pearl Hyde School, Coventry**

# Terror Of The Dragon!

'Ha!' said Darren, 'that dragon is the size of my ...
help! Get it off now! It's killing me!' he screamed.
'Hello Darren,' said his mum, 'how do you like
your pet Gecko?'
'But it's a fierce dragon!'
'Honey,' called Mum, 'call the doctor. He's had
hallucinations ... again!'

**Janmatthew Maganga (8)**
**Pearl Hyde School, Coventry**

# House Of Horror

I walked into a house and saw a skull and a dead
body. I screamed as loud as I could, but it was too
late for me. Then someone came in and rescued
me from the house of death.

**Ben Gordon (11)**
**Pewsey Primary School, Pewsey**

# Christmas Robber

*Thud!* 'What's down there?' I said. I went down
to find out. The room was dark and deserted,
there was another thud from the tree. A man in
a Father Christmas outfit stealing all the presents.
'Ho, ho, ho,' the man cheered. I quickly ran
upstairs. 'Yikes! Christmas already!'

**Ollie Dodson (11)**

**Pewsey Primary School, Pewsey**

# Never!

I walked through the trees, to the meadow,
and saw a horrific fight. Two wolves snapped at
each other, until one surrendered. Suddenly the
winning wolf was a boy of twelve, staring at me. 'I
said I would come back.'
'You don't love anyone else?'
Disbelievingly. 'Never!' I vowed.

**Charlotte Pullin (10)**
**Pewsey Primary School, Pewsey**

# Boo!

'And here is the 10 o'clock News,' screamed the
TV as I turned it on. *Slam!* The door shuts after
my parents.
Five minutes later, the doorbell rings. 'Who is it?'
I creep up to the door. Suddenly the door swings
open …
'Boo! Now for your birthday surprise.'

**Lydia Tannasee (11)**
**Pewsey Primary School, Pewsey**

# Haunted By The Devil

Spotted the manor on the corner of Gothic Avenue. I cautiously walked in! The glass mysteriously smashed! I heard the door creak slowly! My heart was thumping madly! I saw the Devil glaring at me suspiciously! He grabbed me around the neck! The lights flickered vigorously! I collapsed!

**Charlie Ward (11)**
Pewsey Primary School, Pewsey

# H-Force

The hamsters were in their secret den in the sofa.
They were planning to break into the local bank.
Were they planning to steal money or kidnap the
workers?
So the next day they ran along to the bank and
they shouted, 'Put your hands up.' They stole
£280,000.

**Jacques Draper (10)**
**Pewsey Primary School, Pewsey**

# My Fate Has Come ...

I was walking across a bridge, it snapped in half. I was falling to my death! Out of the blue a dragon popped out of nowhere and caught me on his back. The dragon and I travelled through the air and I turned the next page of my book.

**Luke Helps (10)**
**Pewsey Primary School, Pewsey**

# Eek!

I walked into a dark, gloomy house, I heard rats
screeching, the floorboards creaking, piercing
screams echoed the halls. Walking the endless
corridors, reaching out for light … Suddenly the
door began to shake. I screeched, 'Eek!'
As the door flew open a voice spoke. 'Hey
Sophie, wanna play out?' Phew!

**Emma Lucy Spence-Hirst (11)**
**Pewsey Primary School, Pewsey**

# In The Navy

The whole house was mourning for their dad,
for Milly a dad, and husband for Katrina. He was
going off to WWII. He had no choice. He kissed
Milly and Katrina goodbye, got on the train. As
he pressed his delicate nose against the window,
Milly murmured, 'Goodbye Daddy, farewell.'

**Ethan Fishlock (9)**
**Pewsey Primary School, Pewsey**

# The Great Mystery

Off they go, speeding away. Earlier Jack placed
a bet on the currently second-placed Audi but
in first, heading into the final lap, the Aston goes
over the hill and is never seen again. Leaving the
dreaded Audi to win.
What is that shadow on the hill?
What happened?

**Christopher Hargreaves (9)**
Pewsey Primary School, Pewsey

102

# Spooks!

I walked into the mansion, the door creaked
and slowly screeched open. The floorboards
squeaked, the glass smashed, I jumped. Suddenly I
could hear rats were closing in on me. I could see
cobwebs in every corner, I heard voices. I ducked
down.
'Boo!'
I fell out of bed.

**Ryan Granger (11)**
**Pewsey Primary School, Pewsey**

# Dolphin Dreams With A Bit Of Horror

I fell into a deep sleep and the next thing I knew
I was swimming with beautiful dolphins, in the
Hawaiian sea!
After a while the dolphins swam off! I looked
behind me to see what scared them off and I
suddenly saw it, a great big, white, scary shark!

**Morgan Cooper (10)**
Pewsey Primary School, Pewsey

# Exploring Hamster

The hamster was getting fatter and fatter as his vampire owners were feeding him way too much. Each and every day the poor, but greedy, hamster grew larger and larger, then shorter and very, very chubby.

After two weeks of being with the vampires, he got so fat he exploded … !

**Hannah-Louise Eells (9)**

**Pewsey Primary School, Pewsey**

# The Football Dream

The boy was playing his first match of football for United. He gets the ball on the wing, runs into the box and the keeper comes out. The boy lobs the keeper and scores. The crowd goes wild, but then he wakes up, and it is all a dream.

**Morgan Plank (10)**

**Pewsey Primary School, Pewsey**

# The Horror And Dare Game!

One day there was a girl called Gemma. Gemma
had friends called Cheryl and Marci. Cheryl had a
dare and horror game. Gemma played it and she
got eaten. So Marci had a go and she killed them
all! If Gemma really died it would be very scary
and sad.

**Emily Tapper (9)**
**Pewsey Primary School, Pewsey**

107

# Help Me

'They are after me!' I screamed, trying to find a knife.
'I know where you are,' the voice followed me.
I seemed to be shaking, he took the knife from my hand. I reached for the torch. I shone it in his bloodthirsty eyes …
'Cut!' said the director.

**Caitlin Pegg (10)**
Pewsey Primary School, Pewsey

# The Flying Man

Max was riding along on his motorbike when two
beautiful golden wings shot out of his back. He
started to rise then Max was flying over the sea.
Suddenly his wings disappeared. Was this the end?

**Douglas Tannasee (9)**
Pewsey Primary School, Pewsey

# Emma's Dream

One night Emma was dreaming about horses. She was galloping through the field amongst a shimmering lake. The sun was out and shining down on Emma and her beautiful black stallion. Then they stopped down by the lake. What was happening? Suddenly her horse disappeared ... Was it all a dream?

**Tonisha Rowe (9)**
Pewsey Primary School, Pewsey

# The Dream

Out in the snow were two girls called Alice and
Bella. Bella was a newborn vampire. All of a
sudden, out in the darkness, leapt Victoria. Alice
cried, 'Bella, run!'
Jacob appeared, he ripped the head off of
Victoria, and Bella escaped without a scratch.

**Erin McKay (10)**
**Pewsey Primary School, Pewsey**

# The Lost Polar Bear

On the ice, in Antarctica, there was a mum polar
bear, who told baby polar bear to stay out of
danger.
One day the little polar bear went for an
adventure through the Antarctic ice. Suddenly the
ice began to break, so he ran back to his mum.

**Abi Ward (9)**
**Pewsey Primary School, Pewsey**

# Untitled

The agent jumped into the enemy base and shot two guards with his trusty guns, then crept slowly and quietly into the boss' room where the master was. It was face to face. The master shot him ... Would he die?

**Ethan Lee (9)**
Pewsey Primary School, Pewsey

# Out Of The Window

He looked out the window to see thousands of
stars outside. He jumped out of his bed in horror
and shouted to his mum. His mum asked what
the matter was, and she rushed up the stairs. She
saw the curtains, 'You silly Billy,' she said, pulling
the curtains open.

**Phoebe Young (9)**
**Pewsey Primary School, Pewsey**

# The World's Last Hope

The evil dolphins teamed up with Pegasus, then went to destroy the world! But Danny and Armoured Penguin swapped them with their machine gun, plus pistol. Then a giant sea monster attacked. Danny and Armoured Penguin had to call for back-up.

**Dan Pocock (9)**
**Pewsey Primary School, Pewsey**

# The Dark Room

Clenching my fists I entered the dark room, then suddenly the door slammed behind me. I felt a hand clench on my shoulder. I felt a tear of sweat run down the side of my cheek, then suddenly I blacked out.
I woke in bed, was it a dream?

**Haydn Spicer (10)**
**Pewsey Primary School, Pewsey**

# The Mercenary And The Suicide Bombers

There was a man who ruled the west side of
England. He started a company called, the suicide
bombers. The man who ruled was called Jack.
The queen of the Eastern side started a war. The
queen hired a mercenary called Doug to kill Jack
and he did!

**Max Knight (10)**
Pewsey Primary School, Pewsey

# The Haunted House

Starr went home to a gloomy house. There was
a table with cards on. Suddenly some gnomes
appeared and laughed. Starr sat at the table,
surprisingly it started to spin. The table lifted,
Starr whacked her head. At that point she knew it
was all a dream. What happened?

**Rowan Norcliffe (9)**

**Pewsey Primary School, Pewsey**

# Death Is Coming

The two boys ignored their mum and went in the deep, dark, dangerous old mine. As they went deeper, something deadly got closer and closer … No one knows what happened next. Legend said they died a horrible death!

**Charlie Charles Peberdy-Feuillebois (10)**
Pewsey Primary School, Pewsey

# MI High Agents

There is a school, not far away, where spies are
tracking down the bad guys. We are called MI
High Agents. My agents are called Rose, Carry
and Osca, they have really cool gadgets. Our base
is underground, we have a strict teacher called
Miss King. We like our job.

**Angel Elzubaidy (10)**
**Pewsey Primary School, Pewsey**

# The Twin

I walked towards the door of my house. It creaked open. I walked in. I heard funny but strange voices. They sounded like aliens. Slowly I crept into the room. 'Hello!'
I jumped.
'Hello twin!' said my brother playing on his Xbox.

**William Bateman (11)**
**Portreath Community Primary School, Portreath**

# Mr Muggins

Mr Muggins walked down the path, before
sliding over a banana and falling on his back. He
wondered if this was a plot set up by Mr Muggins
of Scalextric who organised this trap before he
came down the path. He went on the trail ...

**Thomas Bateman (11)**
Portreath Community Primary School, Portreath

# The Dark And Deserted House

The house was dark and appeared deserted when
Dom arrived home. *How strange*, he thought.
I'm sure Mum and Dad said they would be here.
A sudden creak, a man jumped out and grabbed
him, but he used his Kung Fu skills to get him off
and he kicked him.

**Dominic Hill (11)**
**Portreath Community Primary School, Portreath**

123

# The Surprise Birthday

I was woken by a loud noise coming from downstairs. I was trembling as I stepped silently downstairs. As I reached the bottom I cautiously tiptoed down the hall into the living room, Suddenly the light came on blinding me. All I heard was, 'Surprise,' then after that, 'Happy birthday.'

**Leonie Walker (11)**

Portreath Community Primary School, Portreath

124

# A Vicious Viking

I opened the door and there, standing menacingly,
was a vicious Viking with a double-handed axe
in his large, muscly hand. I trembled, I shook, I
panicked, but I had no fear of a Viking warrior.
'Boo!' I bellowed, bravely and the vicious Viking
fled screaming into the distance.

**Javier Gomez (9)**
**Portreath Community Primary School, Portreath**

# Face To Face

Suddenly there I was, face to face with the most beautiful thing I'd ever seen - the coral reef. All the magnificent fish and coral there were to see. All the pinks and greens and blue, all the seaweed rocking to and fro. The shimmer of the sun is amazing.

**Eve Prout (9)**

Portreath Community Primary School, Portreath

# The Lost Pet

I got home from school and with its tail tucked under a plant pot there, miaowing like mad, was a kitten with cuts all over it. I took it to the vet and they said we could keep her. We called her Ella. Ella lived with us till she died.

**Elise Laity (10)**
Portreath Community Primary School, Portreath

# The Adventure Of Storm!

Once upon a time there was a boy named Storm.
He lived with his mother and father in a town
called Falconreach.
One day an evil bandit came to take everyone's
gold. The people said if he was beaten, in battle,
he couldn't have the gold. 'I'll fight,' declared
Storm ...

**Luke Spare (11)**
Portreath Community Primary School, Portreath

# The Dam!

As the Lancaster swooped towards the dam,
a layer of machine gun bullets came charging
towards it! The bomb aimer smashed down on
the button and the bomb dropped and skipped
over the water! They saw the dam explode into a
million pieces; and the water whooshed through
the breech!

**James Chant (10)**
**Portreath Community Primary School, Portreath**

# Spilt Milk

I was awakened by the sound of my front gate
squeaking as it opened. I looked at my clock, it
was only 4am. Suddenly I heard the sound of
smashing glass. I crept out of bed and looked out
of my window, guess what I saw. The Milkman!

**Dylan Nash (10)**

Portreath Community Primary School, Portreath

# Oliver's Mum Went To America

*Ding-dong* the bell went. Oliver Mitchell went to answer it and it was his mother. She had been away for a year. She had been to America. He was pleased to see her. She went there to see her parents who were ill. She had really missed her son.

**Leah Robins (8)**

**Portreath Community Primary School, Portreath**

# The Scary Story

I opened the door and saw it. A vampire, zombie
and a dwarf. The vampire anxiously roared. The
zombie started walking towards me and was
about to grab me, but I ran away and shouted,
'Help!' Luckily my next-door-neighbour heard
me, but I remembered it was Halloween.

**Luke Giles (11)**
Portreath Community Primary School, Portreath

132

# Warehouse Wonders

Feeling uneasy, Megan wandered into the warehouse. *That's odd,* she thought, *I'm sure Kiera told me to meet her here.*
The warehouse seemed eerie and uninviting. Megan was positive that something was lurking, watching her. A sudden noise startled her. 'Surprise!' Megan breathed a sigh of relief. A surprise party.

**Elke Youlton (11)**
**Portreath Community Primary School, Portreath**

# Pirate Panic!

Herbert was feared by every buccaneer along
Cornwall's craggy coastline. Herbert was hairy
where everyone else wasn't! Also, he lived on a
diet of trout and mustard, eels and custard.
One day, he sent out invitations to the pirate
population. They read: 'Ballerina ball, pink dresses
for all.'
*'Argh! Panic!'*

**Oliver Johnson (10)**
**Portreath Community Primary School, Portreath**

# The Treasure Map

Jack jumped out of bed and rushed outside to dig up his time capsule. Suddenly the spade hit something hard, what was it? He started digging frantically. He looked down and saw a wooden box. He carefully lifted the lid and to his amazement he found an old treasure map.

**Madeleine Thomas (10)**
Portreath Community Primary School, Portreath

# A Magical Place

Cautiously I stepped over the threshold of the garden gate. A powerful odour reached my nostrils; it was delicious. Flourishing bushes, plants and trees lay before me in lightly mowed grass and compost. The vulnerable birds in their delicate nests twittered away to each other. This was a magical place.

**Belén Gomez (11)**
Portreath Community Primary School, Portreath

136

# Disasters In The Dark

My feet carried me as fast as they could down the
gloomy alleyway. Leaping like a lion, the ghostly
silhouette wouldn't capitulate. With my heart still
pounding, I felt faint. 'Trick or treat?' shouted the
ghostly figure. To my surprise it was my older
brother trying out his Halloween outfit!

**Erin Mitchell (10)**
**Portreath Community Primary School, Portreath**

# The True Story Of Humpty-Dumpty

Humpty-Dumpty wanted to be a soldier but
he was too round. He tried to get the king's
attention so he climbed on top of a wall! As he
marched along he fell off. So all the king's horses
and all the king's men had tasty scrambled eggs
for breakfast!

**Kathleen Murtagh (8)**

St Francis Catholic Primary School, Ascot

138

# The Rattlesnake

It was the end of our first day at Disneyland
and I was exhausted, soaking wet but happy. A
hurricane was starting. Suddenly I saw a crowd
of people and heard screaming. 'What now?
Through the crowd we saw it - a huge rattlesnake
heading in our direction!
'Run!' Mum said.

**Saffron Fearn (8)**
St Francis Catholic Primary School, Ascot

# The Lost Colours

The elves and fairies of Rainbow Kingdom gathered in the courtyard worriedly. Veronica and Storm, the dark unicorn, had stolen the colours and turned everything and everyone grey. However, then Heidi and Scarlett, the white Pegasus, flew down with the rainbow wand and restored the colours, saving the day again.

**Lois McGuire (7)**

St Francis Catholic Primary School, Ascot

140

# Monster

My eyes opened. It was morning. There was a big light. It was terrifying! I took a glance through the curtains. What was it? it was a monster! My eyes were drawn to it, it came closer and closer. There was a tremendous roar, the monster ran away. Peaceful again!

**Jan Heitplatz (7)**
**St Francis Catholic Primary School, Ascot**

# Poppy's Adventure

Poppy's favourite adventure was in America. Her adventure started when she went to a party. It was a sleepover party. She met her friend that she hadn't seen for ages. She was so happy that she asked if she could stay, the girl said, yes. The adventure began.

**Grace Scott (7)**

**St Francis Catholic Primary School, Ascot**

142

# The Ghost In Beanotown!

Once there was a boy called Ryan. 'What shall I do today?' he said. In the meantime it was getting dark, he was looking for friends. It got dark so he went to sleep. Suddenly he had a nightmare, a ghost, 'Argh!' no one ever saw him again.

**Ryan Reid (8)**
St Francis Catholic Primary School, Ascot

# Miranda's Mysterious Rabbit

One day Miranda bought a white fluffy rabbit. She
cuddled her so much she called her Snuggles.
At night Snuggles' eyes turned very red and her
teeth became fangs. She bit into Miranda's neck
until it bled and she became a vampire. So you'd
better watch out!

**Jada-Lei Titre (8)**
St Francis Catholic Primary School, Ascot

# Over The Edge

I was passing Nursery Town Hill when I noticed my friends Jack and Jill at the top. 'Hi' I shouted. Distracted, Jack stumbled and fell all the way down the slope. To my amazement Jill followed. There was blood everywhere. Luckily I had a supply of vinegar and brown paper.

**Joseph Martin (8)**
St Francis Catholic Primary School, Ascot

# Friends

The boy went to the park. He had lots of fun with his friends because the game was so good. He saw a ball so he wanted to play with the ball but his friends didn't want to play. Then they thought playing with the ball was the best ever.

**Ben McCluskey (8)**

St Francis Catholic Primary School, Ascot

# Samurai Sam

Once there was a man named Sam. He thought
he was ordinary but soon he found out he had
Samurai powers. He went to a Samurai training
academy to have fun, then he got attacked. He
fought evil valiantly and won with his friends Bob,
Jim and Fred. Hooray!

**Niall Milner (9)**
St Francis Catholic Primary School, Ascot

# The Story Of The Phantom Postman

It was a dark and stormy night where wolves were howling. A postman called Henry strode up the front path of a mansion. He tried to deliver his letters through the gaping mouth of the letter box, but he will never deliver them. Henry is the phantom postman!

**Matthew Ringshaw (9)**

St Francis Catholic Primary School, Ascot

# The Creature

One day a sad, old man walked down a dark and twisty road. Suddenly a creature scratched him across the heart. He dialled 999. When the ambulance arrived he had vanished. All they found was a bloody T-shirt.
To this day no one knows where he is. Only the creature knows.

### Sebastian Parnham (8)
**St Francis Catholic Primary School, Ascot**

149

# The Life Of A Fairy

Hello, my name's Andrea. I'm a rose fairy but I've always wanted to be a human. Yesterday I went into a hole that led to the human world. There was a house nearby, I went inside a squirrel hole and I saw that it was a human. I went back.

**Marie-Louise Lawson (8)**
St Francis Catholic Primary School, Ascot

# Untitled

One day Jim and Joe woke up to a strange day.
Jim and Joe went downstairs and sat on the new
sofa bed. They fell through it and landed in a
Celtic valley. Two boys were staring at them, they
said the Romans were getting ready to invade!

**Peter Wall (9)**
**St Francis Catholic Primary School, Ascot**

# Why Penguins Can't Fly

Penguins have always been very beautiful, so they became extremely vain. The king of the birds demanded, 'Stop showing off or suffer the consequences.' The silly penguins were too busy preening themselves to hear him. This angered the king, who cursed them, so now they are still beautiful but flightless.

**Ava Murtagh (10)**
St Francis Catholic Primary School, Ascot

# First Contact

*Hiss … ! Zipp … ! Clang … !* The door of the capsule opened and a huge cloud of gas engulfed the landing site … When the cloud cleared, out came a minuscule robotic dog called S A M or Special Agent Max. He scanned the landscape to detect the microchipped bone. At last there it was!

**Jack Cullen (9)**
St Francis Catholic Primary School, Ascot

# Night Tales

I read the headline! The lost will had to be found!
My mind was on the conversation, is it related?
The strange men were whispering, 'Heart, will,
the abandoned mansion.'
'The heart of the mansion is the cellar, the will
must be there! I will go at dead of night ...'

### Hannah Heitplatz (10)
St Francis Catholic Primary School, Ascot

154

# Strange Sounds

Jim was happily playing, when suddenly he heard noises, scary ones. Jim sprinted very fast but soon, to his horror, he came to a dead end! He leapt into a tree and hid. He peered down. He forgot all safety. After a tumble Jim noticed a radio. 'Not another trick!'

**Gabriela Griffiths (9)**

**St Francis Catholic Primary School, Ascot**

# Frankie And The Turban Towel

Frankie loves swimming and enjoys laughing and playing out. Her hair is one of the most precious pieces. When she comes out of the pool, she wraps her fine gorgeous hair in a spotted turban towel, round her hair and suddenly …

**Maddison Cullimore (10)**
St Francis Catholic Primary School, Ascot

# The Day I Became A Superhero

One day I was playing football with my friends at the park. I was the goalkeeper, one of my friends shot in the far corner, so I dived to try and save it. Then suddenly I flew through the air. I realised I could fly! So now I'm a superhero.

**Kai Eves-Hollis (10)**

St Francis Catholic Primary School, Ascot

# Untitled

Tom wanted to get tickets to watch 'Dragons' in
the cinema, but it was sold out.
One day he was walking along the street and he
saw a bit of paper by the drain, he picked it up
and saw it was a ticket, he had got one!

**Robert Linch (10)**
St Francis Catholic Primary School, Ascot

158

# Haunted

Once there was a deserted house which
everyrone said was haunted. Lilly wanted to
prove it wasn't, so she went in one night and she
heard a big creak. She turned around and there
was a little mouse.
From then on she played in the house every day.

**Ellena Collins (9)**
St Francis Catholic Primary School, Ascot

# The Big Match

Today we went to the World Cup Final. Brazil Vs
England. The match kicked off and Brazil took
the early lead. I was bursting with excitement.
England kept battling hard and finally scored.
Suddenly they scored another. England were
victorious once again. Everyone felt amazingly
proud of the England team.

**Matthew Daniels (9)**

St Francis Catholic Primary School, Ascot

# Creepy Sounds

One night while Katy was sleeping, she heard a
strange sound downstairs. She crept down the
stairs to investigate but ran back up to her room
as she heard the sound again. Feeling brave she
peeped downstairs one more time. Silly Katy! It
was only Mum and Dad watching TV!

**Abbe Docherty (10)**
**St Francis Catholic Primary School, Ascot**

# A Glimpse Of Super Stardom

Lights and cameras in front of you. Paparazzi
surrounding you. Rubbish news in magazines. This
is not what I wanted super stardom to be. I guess
it's hard to be a celebrity, all the glitz and glam,
it's not that easy.

**Olivia Kline (10)**

St Francis Catholic Primary School, Ascot

# SATs

The questions kept coming. What is a quarter of eight? Write three quarters as a decimal. Panic filled me and I scribbled out the first answer I could think of. Shaking nervously I waited for the next question.
One day I promised to smash the mental maths CD forever!

**Maddy Brant (9)**
**St Francis Catholic Primary School, Ascot**

# When Teddy Bears Attack

The house was empty except for a few teddy bears. It was a full moon night. Then a sudden green light erupted from the middle of the house. Teddy bears ran at windows, the shards of glass got stuck in the teddies' behinds. 'To the village!' screamed a teddy bear.

**Conor Murphy (11)**

St Francis Catholic Primary School, Ascot

# The Mad Professor

There once was a mad professor. As you heard
he's mad! His last invention, the bouncy stick,
blew up Wales! The testers were coming to see
his new invention. A robot! (How many things
can go wrong). The robot rolled up to them and
pulled out semi machine guns. *Bang!*

**Sean Murphy (11)**
**St Francis Catholic Primary School, Ascot**

# Alien-Napped

I looked out my bedroom window and saw it
… a metallic object gleamed in the moonlight, a
spaceship! Cautiously, I crept down the stairs and
went into the garden. Grassy-green men plodded
out the ship. Suddenly they grabbed me and I was
whisked away far in the universe.

**Archie White (11)**
St Francis Catholic Primary School, Ascot

# A Cinderella Story

There was a girl called Cinderella, all she wanted
was a fella. She married a prince, a handsome
man and thought she would be his number one
fan. But it turned out he was not right, so she
found a baker, a famous cookie maker, and lived
happily ever after.

**Erin McPhee (10)**
**St Francis Catholic Primary School, Ascot**

# The Cat Search

I've searched far and wide for my cat - I've really tried - through the woods, down the lane, through both sunshine and the rain. A log collapsed over the stream, I looked inside the hollow tree, you'd never guess what I could see? It was my cat, I grinned with glee!

**Natasha Sadowski (10)**
St Francis Catholic Primary School, Ascot

168

# How I Saved The World

It was the end of the world, everything was on fire! Then I saw the key that Doctor Evil had used to unlock 'The Box of Death'. I grabbed the key and closed the box, everything stopped! But Doctor Evil was getting away. I ran and jumped on him!

**Owen Milner (11)**
**St Francis Catholic Primary School, Ascot**

# Deserted

The footsteps were getting louder and louder as
the hooded person got closer. I stood helpless,
just hoping that the person would not kill me! But
while I'd been thinking something had crept up on
me. It seized me. Held me tight and sunk his fangs
into me ...

**Abigail Waters (11)**
St Francis Catholic Primary School, Ascot

# The Monster

I was in the park when it happened, a big, green, gooey monster grabbed me and held me up in the air. I managed to escape and jump down but it wasn't over. I noticed a red button on the back of its leg. I pressed it. He tumbled down.

**Callum Laney (10)**
St Francis Catholic Primary School, Ascot

# Top Gear Get Fined

Welcome to the Top Gear track. Oh what's that?
The Ferrari FXX is being driven by the ultimate
Stig round the course! Oh no he's whizzed out of
control! He's power sliding ... *crash!*
Top Gear have to pay an extremely high £1.3m
for Ferrari to make a new one.

**Matthew D'Agata (10)**

**St Francis Catholic Primary School, Ascot**

# Pigs Can Fly

One summer's day, Harry was sunbathing outside
his mansion and something was coming out of the
clouds. A flying pig! Harry immediately jumped
in his pool. He looked back up and it was his
imagination, everyone laughed at him.

**Michael Balfour (11)**
**St Francis Catholic Primary School, Ascot**

# Lucy And The Forest's Ferny Floor

Lucy was playing hide-and-seek in a forest with her friends when the forest's ferny floor started to swallow her up. She was struggling and screaming, but no one came. It was just her. As the leaves were swallowing her up she suddenly heard a rustling noise ...

**Catherine Vandenberg (11)**

St Francis Catholic Primary School, Ascot

# Tim

Tim loved cakes, all cakes; Pink cakes, shiny cakes and lots more. He went to the park and saw a car crash through the park gates, aiming straight for a shopping trolley. A baby was in the trolley, but Tim saw cakes, he ran to save the cakes … but failed!

**Robert Humphrey (10)**
St Francis Catholic Primary School, Ascot

# Bush Monster

One dark night, Tommas was walking home from school, a guy came out and beat him up! Who was it? The police searched everywhere, they found the person who killed him and put him in jail.

**Robbie Greenwood (11)**
St Francis Catholic Primary School, Ascot

# Trapped

The door creaked, then slammed shut. *Bang!*
The wind whispered in a strange manner. It was
a ghost! I swallowed and strode forward, trying
not to be scared. A black-hooded figure floated in
mid-air and then disappeared. I struggled to reach
the switch and stumbled - I was trapped!

**Charlotte De Speville (10)**
**St Francis Catholic Primary School, Ascot**

# The Coke Bottle

The clumsy Coke bottle sat on a bridge, waiting
for someone to tip him over. For days and days
nobody came, until one boy came. Hooray! the
Coke bottle fell to the depths of the river, doing
flips and twists the whole way down. He reached
the bottom and died.

**Jacob Daniels (11)**

St Francis Catholic Primary School, Ascot

# Stroppy Suzie

Suzie was out with Dad, they were in a car and
had been travelling all day when Suzie saw a horse
in hay. 'I want horsey! I'll die if I don't!'
'You won't!'
But that night Suzie wouldn't eat dinner and got
thinner until, in despair, she died.

**Sofia Thomas (11)**
St Francis Catholic Primary School, Ascot

# House Of Horrors

As I cautiously stepped into the ghost house,
I whizzed away into the darkness. Suddenly
millions of tiny lights clicked on and off. Without
warning, two axes dropped from the ceiling,
my journey had begun! Skeleton after skeleton
chased me through the ghost house. 'Well, at
least it's over now!'

**Bailey Graham (10)**
St Francis Catholic Primary School, Ascot

# The Dark And Stormy Night

It was a dark and stormy night. Everything was cold and scary. I felt I was being followed. There were bats all around me. Suddenly I tripped and fell into a big hole as the wind fluttered up in my face like a butterfly. Then I woke. What a dream!

**Amy Ringshaw (8)**
St Francis Catholic Primary School, Ascot

# Pop!

*Pop!* James opened a packet of crisps but the wrong way round, so they all fell out. He went to buy a packet of sweets. When he got out of the shop he opened them. Unfortunately they had gone.
Meanwhile a man was eating them. 'Oh no!' exclaimed James.

**Benjamin Cook (10)**
St Francis Catholic Primary School, Ascot

# Alone

It was a dark and gloomy night, owls hooted and wolves howled. Sam didn't like the sound of it at all! With one twist Sam was alone. Shivering bones Sam saw that he was being followed. Each step he took he could hear someone else's. Sam looked up and saw …

**Krishma Kapoor (11)**
St Francis Catholic Primary School, Ascot

# Untitled

One day I walked to the sweet shop. I bought some Tangfastics, Haribo, Skittles and some Mini Eggs. Meanwhile my brother and my dad were playing football. When we got home Mum said, I had to eat my lunch first, to my disgust. When I finished I ate my sweets.

**Aislinn Kate McGrath (9)**

St Monica's Catholic Primary School, Appleton

# The Scary Monster

As Kate skipped home through the dark, spooky woods some red scary eyes looked at her through the green bushes. 'Argh!' it jumped out at her and Kate screamed. It looked like a little dog. Oops, it was her little dog after all. Kate and Bonnie raced each other home.

**April Geary (10)**
St Monica's Catholic Primary School, Appleton

# Untitled

One morning the three bears went out on an adventure. They were all really looking forward to it but when they came back their house had been wrecked. They found an unmade bed, a broken chair and an empty bowl. The three bears wished that they had tidied up earlier!

**Morgan Unsworth (9)**
St Monica's Catholic Primary School, Appleton

# The Mini Egg

Janet eagerly glared at the sapphire speckled
chicken egg. The mini egg started to crack! Janet
felt a tingle that started to grow. She knew this
mini egg was a peacock. What else would it be?
Then *pop*! Out came the cutest … dinosaur! Janet
suddenly said, 'That's my £20 gone.'

**Rebecca Giles (11)**
**The Tynings School, Bristol**

# Midnight Murder

Amy couldn't sleep. Rain hammered down as men's voices echoed around. Suddenly, she heard a knock on the door. Uneasily she crept downstairs. She opened the door, finding herself staring into a stranger's face. He held a dagger. As the blade plunged into her heart, she watched the stranger disappear.

**Maggie Lewis (10)**
The Tynings School, Bristol

# Scary Moment!

*Knock, knock.* The door opened slowly with a
squeaky noise. 'Who's there?' cried Ricky, while
she was shaking to open the door.
There was a scary voice saying, 'It's me, it's me.
I'm back Ricky.'
'Who's that?'
'It's a zombie.'
'Argh!' So she opened the door.
'Surprise, it's me!'

**Amber Smith (10)**
**The Tynings School, Bristol**

# Only A Dream

Sarah was relaxing on the hot, sunny beach.
Suddenly she heard a noise behind her. Turning
around fearfully, an ugly pirate jumped out at her.
'Give me that gold necklace you're wearing!' he
demanded.
'No!' she screamed. There was a huge bang,
Sarah was on the floor beside her bed.

**Michaela Anderson (11)**
**The Tynings School, Bristol**

# Dad, What Are You Doing?

Banging came from outside ... Nicky peered out the window. It was her father digging up Nicky's mum's grave. 'Dad!' yelled Nicky hoping that her dad would stop digging. Dad didn't hear, but in a few seconds, he turned around (because he spotted Nicky) and in a few seconds he'd gone ...

**Lydia Harris (10)**
**The Tynings School, Bristol**

# Halloween Night

It was Halloween night in New York City. Becky wanted to go out with her friends but she had to ask her parents first. 'Mum, Dad?' yelled Becky. 'Yes honey?' replied her mother.
'Can I go out with my friends?' asked Becky. 'Sure,' shouted Becky's dad. Becky couldn't find anyone.

**Cassie Simmons (10)**

**The Tynings School, Bristol**

# Laura's Spooky Moment

There was a gigantic creaky door, which was
peacefully unwanted. Laura walked in through
the gigantic creaky door with a terrifying look,
she was gobsmacked by what was in there. Laura
stamped in shock whilst she walked through.
Then she walked home and told her mother and
father everything.

**Amy Adams (11)**
**The Tynings School, Bristol**

# Cops 'N' Robbers

'Gary get the load!' said Nigel, who was now heaving a brown sack into their silver Volvo. Unwillingly, Gary roared up the engine. Quickly, doing a sharp handbrake turn to the M1. Minutes after, flashing sirens were all around them. Colours flashed into their eyes; madly, they accelerated desperately!

**Rosie Clayton Richards (11)**
**The Tynings School, Bristol**

# Odysseus And The Cool Cyclops

In 487BC Odysseus was cruising on a ferry,
shaving his brown beard.
Finally, they arrived at the deserted island where
the cyclops lived. When they went in his cave,
they saw him groaning to the beat. 'Hey!' said the
cyclops, 'Join in.'
'We will!' Odysseus replied. They had fun!

**Elliott Merrifield (11)**

**The Tynings School, Bristol**

# Mysterious Figure

*Smash!* The gigantic yellow door slammed open -
a beastly white figure emerged at the door! It was
a ghost! As fast as Emily could she dashed forth
for the door to try to close it but sadly the figure
walked through. 'Argh!' Emily lay there on the
floor, blood squirting everywhere.

**Daniel Thresher (11)**

**The Tynings School, Bristol**

# Attic Scare

'Mum, I'm gonna take a peek in our attic!' I yelled
as I shot up the stairs. I crept into the deserted
attic, I heard creaks on the floorboards as wafts of
dust came flying past me. Something grabbed my
shoulder. 'Boo!' Thomas screamed. I flew down
the stairs.

**Emily Silverthorn (10)**
**The Tynings School, Bristol**

# Who's There?

Suddenly the door creaked open. Sarah jumped
from her bed. 'Who's there?' whispered Sarah.
She ran as fast as she could to her mum and dad.
'Where are you?' Sarah said quietly.
'Ha, ha, ha, ha' an evil laugh came out of
someone. That person was nowhere to be seen.

**Laura Hall (11)**
The Tynings School, Bristol

# King Henry VIII

King Henry VIII smashed his way through the
dining doors. Edward the VI was lying in his cot
and Mary was about to drop a wooden block
on his head. 'What do you think you are doing?'
Henry screamed.
Edward started to cry.
'I shall behead you for this!'

**Maxmillian Morch-Monsted (10)**

**The Tynings School, Bristol**

# 50 Word Story

I went on holiday to a forest. I was looking for some animals in the forest. I found a monkey in the tree so I went again. I found a lion and a frog and I went back home.

**Adrian Hudd (11)**
**The Tynings School, Bristol**

# The Demon Toothbrush

Alan peeped round the corner of the bathroom.
His mouth dropped open as he saw an enormous
toothbrush levitate, then fall to the floor as
Alan made his presence clear. He picked up the
toothbrush. There was a small piece of paper on
it; 'Welcome to the house of doom!'

**Timothy Pike (10)**
**The Tynings School, Bristol**

# The Tudors

In Tudor times there was a man named Henry
VIII and he was a king. He had six wives but there
was a catch. He told them that he wanted a boy
but all he got was girls. So he decided to divorce,
behead and kill six women.

**Sam Hawkins (11)**
**The Tynings School, Bristol**

# The Mystery Of The Ghost Onslaught

*Whollup!* The rusty door boomed open as if it was loose. A mysterious figure emerged whistling through the abandoned slaughter house with blood and brains all over the manky wall. The mysterious figure had dried-blood-smudged fangs as if it had just slaughtered someone ... Had it?

**Matthew Pepworth (11)**
**The Tynings School, Bristol**

# The Bungee Trampoline

Bob had a go on a bungee trampoline. 'This is really cool!' he shouted down to his mum.
'Can I have a go?' his little sister said.
'No, you are too young, maybe next year,' said her mum.
'Hey guys, are you swaying?' yelled Bob.
'Small bit,' Mum yelled back.

**Elvi Fraser (9)**
Tough School, Alford

# The Loch Ness Monster

I was walking along the edge of Loch Ness when suddenly I heard a splash. I turned around to see the Loch Ness monster. It swam right up to me. I climbed on its back and we swam away together and lived happily ever after in a dark, cosy cave.

**Alice Hepburn (10)**
Tough School, Alford

# Manchester United

Vidic passes to Carrick, Carrick runs, Aston
Villa defends, passes to Owen and shoots in the
bottom corner, 'Goal!'
Second half: Man United have a corner. Giggs fires
it low, Wayne Rooney does a diving header, the
goalkeeper misses the punch and it's Manchester
United 2, Aston Villa 1.

**Kevin Low (9)**
**Tough School, Alford**

Tiny Treasures Tales From Great Britain

# The Crash

As Schumacher raced round the hammerhead in
first place, his teammate and rival, Massa, came
round to see Schumacher spin off the track. The
petrol was gushing out of his tank. Massa braked
and ran out of his car, then drags Shumacher out
of his car just before … Bang!

**Eddi Fraser (10)**
**Tough School, Alford**

# The Piece Of Solitary Sheet Music

A long time ago a girl ambled through the Atacama desert, when a solitary piece of sheet music, belonging to Harold Wilson, floated to her. The girl picked it up and brought it to an auction and sold it for £90 and 3 shillings. So she relocated to Zanzibar.

**Lauren Howes (11)**
Tough School, Alford

# The Day The World Stopped Turning

There were screams bellowing in my ears, car alarms bleeping, everyone struggling to stay on the ground as the force from the sun's gravity was getting stronger. Everything in sight was burning into ashes and gently floating up into space. Then there was a flash. Standstill. The Earth had ended.

**Craig Pirie (11)**
Tough School, Alford

# A Dream

*Click-clack.* The swords glinted in the fading sun. a scream of pain, a squirt of blood and the swords clattered to the floor. Then … silence. I jolted upright. My brow was wet with cold sweat. That's when I realised it was all a dream. I rolled over and slept.

**Grace Hepburn (12)**
**Tough School, Alford**

# An Extra Surprise

I was having a great birthday party! Suddenly I
heard some heavy breathing. I looked behind
me and I realised it was coming from the closet.
I cautiously walked towards the door. Slowly
opening the door …
*'Roarrgh!'*
A horrible monster came out and started
attacking people. Nobody survived that day!

**Murray Clark (11)**
Tough School, Alford

# The Sheep Who Never Finished School

One day Mary took her sheep to school. It played in the garden until out came Mrs Thompson with a skipping rope.
She had roast lamb for tea that night!

**Lily Woods (10)**
Tower Primary School, Ware

# The Number Fish That Bit My Finger

1, 2, 3, 4, 5 … counting the fish I caught, 6, 7, 8, 9, 10. I let the 10th one go. My friend asked why I let it go. I said. 'A fish bit my finger.'
She said, 'What finger did it bite?'
'This one on my left. Owww, Mummy.'

**Madison Hemmings (10)**
Tower Primary School, Ware

# A Girl Called Libby

One dull morning a bored Libby skipped downstairs. *Crash!* She fell! Suddenly she heard something, it was talking gold. She decided to search for it.

On her way back Libby banged her head then woke up and it was all a dream. But ... the gold was still in her hand!

**Jade Holt (11)**
**Tower Primary School, Ware**

# Scaring People In The Eiffel Tower

As a ghost scaring people in the Eiffel Tower, I decided to scare my friend Callum. It was a dark, rainy day and I saw him, I thought I would scare him, so I did by making weird noises. I came out and frightened him. He told everyone about me!

**Perry Thomas**
**Tower Primary School, Ware**

# The Wizard

Jane was a powerful wizard, she was the greatest of all, the best in all the wizard world.
One day she swapped bodies with her moany mum and grounded her. Later she went to the pub and the nightclub. Luckily she swapped back before moonlight or she'd be the mum!

**Abby Debnam (10)**
Tower Primary School, Ware

# The Ghost Of The Graveyard

Sydney was in a graveyard hiding behind a tombstone. A ghost tried to kill her. She screamed. Dionne came to the rescue and killed the ghost. Sydney said, 'Thanks.' So there were no ghosts ever again.

**Sydney Knight (10)**
**Tower Primary School, Ware**

# The Last Dance For King Percy

One misty winter's morning Queen Elizabeth and Princess Louise decided to hold a ball. But King Percy said if they did he would kill himself. 'Don't be silly,' said Queen Elizabeth, thinking he was joking. But Princess Louise knew he wasn't. That night King Percy killed himself.

**Geri Baxter (9)**
Tower Primary School, Ware

# The Search For A Pearl

Once upon a time there was a girl called Rosie.
One day she was swimming along, trying to find
an oyster with a pearl. Unfortunately she couldn't
find one anywhere. Luckily she found a fairy who
sprinkled magic dust and made an oyster appear.

**Naima Abdul (7)**
**Tower Primary School, Ware**

# Aliens Attack

Once upon a time there were three spacemen
called Tyler, Max and Leo. One day they went for
a trip in their spaceship to Mars. Unfortunately,
when they arrived on Mars, there were three
thousand aliens. Luckily the three spacemen used
their laser guns to shoot the aliens.

**Leo Maynard (7)**
Tower Primary School, Ware

# Abbi's Adventure

Once upon a time there was a girl called Abbi,
who had a horse called Princess.
One day Abbi went to feed Princess.
Unfortunately Princess was missing. Luckily she
was in a big filled with grass. Finally Abbi got her
back to the stable and rode her and fed her.

**Apiphany Rogers (7)**
Tower Primary School, Ware

# Untitled

Once upon a time there lived a lonely old man.
One day the old man was very sad and upset.
Unfortunately he was so sad he walked to a
dangerous lake nearby and tried to kill himself.
Luckily at first he didn't die. Finally he found
himself with his wife.

**Sue Holloway (9)**
Tower Primary School, Ware

# Untitled

Once upon a time there were three kids and they
lived together. One day Mum said, 'Do you want
to go to the fair?' Unfortunately the car had been
broken down so they couldn't go. Luckily it was
close enough to walk. Finally they had a good
time on the cool rides.

**Lewis Thomas (8)**
Tower Primary School, Ware

223

# The Cute Anteater

Once upon a time there lived a cute hairy anteater.

One day the anteater tripped over a huge rock in the middle of the path. Unfortunately a man ran over the anteater. Luckily the man was a vet and took the anteater to his surgery. Finally the anteater got better.

**Francesca Smith (9)**
**Tower Primary School, Ware**

# Haunted Toadstool Temple

He entered. Then Connor heard something but before he could get out, he saw something in front of him. It was a ghost. Then he remembered the powder and he sprayed it at the ghost. The ghost burst into flames and he got out. Phew!

**Brandon Smith (10)**
**Tower Primary School, Ware**

# Dhruval And His Lucky Day

Once there lived a lovely boy called Dhruval who loved playing cricket. One day he was in a hurry because unfortunately he was late for his cricket practice. Luckily he remembered he had forgotten his bat, so he ran back home to get it. Finally he made it to cricket.

**Dhruval Pawar (8)**
Tower Primary School, Ware

# Reggie's Easter

There once lived a slave called Reggie. He
loved eating so he was the shape of an Easter
egg. Easter time was Reggie's favourite time of
year. Reggie, this year, was going to enter the
competition for eating the most yummy Easter
eggs.

Reggie, won! He was granted a wish!

**Megan Allen (8)**
Tower Primary School, Ware

# Three Fat Boys

Once upon a time there were three fat boys that wanted to get across the bridge, to get some food. A bad-tempered man tried to stop them. So the three fat boys pushed and he fell in the water!

**Ben Casey (11)**
Tower Primary School, Ware

228

# Untitled

Once upon a time there was a little girl called
Lucy, she was sweet.
One day Lucy went to the park. Unfortunately
Lucy fell over and she was crying. Luckily Lucy
wasn't bleeding and had no bruises.
Finally she went home to have her dinner and her
marvellous ice cream.

**Katie McClory (8)**
**Tower Primary School, Ware**

# Information

We hope you have enjoyed reading this book - and that you will continue to enjoy it in the coming years.

If you like reading and writing, drop us a line or give us a call and we'll send you a free information pack. Alternatively visit our website at www.youngwriters.co.uk

Write to:
Young Writers Information,
Remus House,
Coltsfoot Drive,
Peterborough,
PE2 9JX

Tel: (01733) 890066
Email: youngwriters@forwardpress.co.uk